MW00895969

PLANET FIXERS GUIDE

By Amrita Sandhu

www.thedazingaz.com

Copyright Page

 This book is a work of fiction.

Contact Info: www.thedazingaz.com

ISBN:
Hard cover: 978-1-7776355-1-0
Paperback: 978-1-7776355-0-3
Ebook: 978-1-7776355-2-7

Published by:
GoWriteMedia

In loving memory of my husband Jason McIntrye.

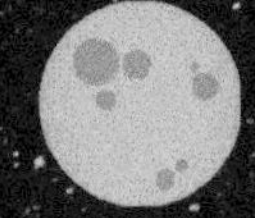
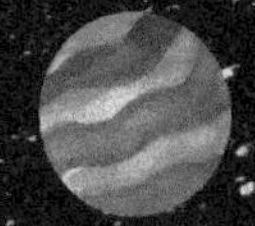

Thank you to my amazing sisters, Sam and Mandy who are my pillars in life.

Thank you Maya and Taran, you inspire me everyday.

Thank you Mom and Dad for keeping me real and letting me always dream big.

Thank you to my editors, Brenda Patterson, Danita Kwong and Judy Heyworth.

Thank you Reggie P...for reminding me to look at the big picture.

Thank you Moai.

...and a shout out to all The Dazingaz fans!

www.thedazingaz.com

Hello, we are the Dazingaz!

Our home planet is called ZigDaz and it had big problems. We worked hard to fix them. Some problems can be fixed quickly while others take more time. Some problems are BIG and others are small.

Always remember that problems have solutions. Take your time working on a problem and if you need help, ask someone that you can trust.

Name: Jinga (JING-a)
Special Interest:
Volunteers to teach sports and exercise
Favorite things:
Sports, dancing, hiking
Favorite food:
Salads, peppermint tea
Personality: Is strong, athletic & adventurous!

Name: Kali (KAL-ee)
Special Interest:
Volunteers to set up clothing and toy donations
Favorite things:
Fashion, jewelry, sunsets and sewing
Favorite food:
Sandwiches
Personality: Is friendly, outgoing & calm!

Name: Zeek (ZEE-k)
Special Interest :
Volunteers at schools to stop bullying and racism
Favorite things:
Music, video games and quiet places
Favorite food:
Pretzels and chocolate milk
Personality: Is sweet, kind and has special needs!

Name: R3 or Re-Ra-Ru (Ree-Ray-Ru)
Special Interest:
Volunteers at schools and companies to help reduce, reuse and recycle
Favorite things:
I like to hide on the pages (can you find me)
Favorite food: Chai tea and lasagna
Personality: Is small, fast and squeaky!

Name: Tago (TAY-go)
Special Interest:
Volunteers to build homes and school
Favorite things:
Working with tools and building things
Favorite food:
Sushi
Personality: Is helpful & understanding!

Name: Seva (SAY-Vah)
Special Interest:
Volunteers to cook, serve and set up food donations
Favorite things:
Trying new recipes and cooking
Favorite food:
Sushi
Personality: Is organized & patient!

Name: Moshi (MO-She)
Special Interest:
Volunteers to keep animals safe and healthy
Favorite things:
Talking with animals and thunderstorms
Favorite food:
Candy and pizza
Personality: Is funny & Can speak every animal language!

Planet Fixers Guide
Chapters

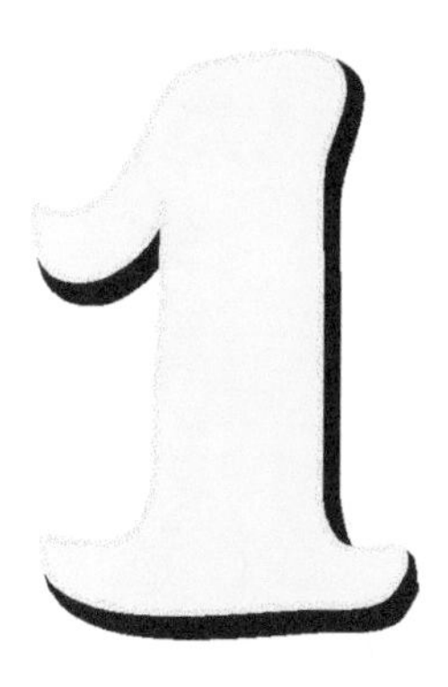

Animals & Pets

"Follow me as we visit a planet that needs help with their pets. I can communicate with every animal in the universe. I love helping animals. I don't just fix the problem but teach pet owners how to be more responsible with their pets."

Dear Moshi

We need your help!

Our pets are very sad. None of them are listening to us. They don't let us eat our dinner and they keep us up all night.

Thank you!
The Mig-Mumps

"Hello, Moshi! Welcome to our planet."

"Thank you Mig-Mumps. What is the problem?"

" It's our pets. They are not happy. Sometimes they are very lazy

and they won't listen to us."

Moshi looked around, "Where are your pets now?"

"Come with us, and we will show you."

Moshi looked up in the trees and saw the Mig-Mumps' pets.

"Do they always hide in the trees and look so sad?" Moshi asked.

"They are spending more and more time up there."

Moshi told the Mig-Mumps to go for a walk. Moshi was going to try and talk with their pets.

Moshi met the Sim-Bob-Ways...

...next the Chirp-Aloos...

...and finally the Min-Nim-Ims.

The Mig-Mumps came back and Moshi explained ...

The Sim-Bob-Ways...need to be fed everyday.

The Chirp-Aloos..need to have fresh water everyday...

...and finally the Min-Nim-Ims need to walk and to play.

Being responsible for your pet means feeding them everyday. If they don't eat they won't have energy. Pets need fresh clean water everyday like you. Finally, being a pet owner means you need to play with them and take them for a walk or run everyday.

Moshi's Pet Checklist

My name: ______________________________

My pet's name: __________________________

- [ ] I have fed my pet today.
- [ ] I have given my pet fresh water today.
- [ ] My pet got exercise today (a walk or run).
- [ ] My pet got a hug from me (maybe not fish).
- [ ] I played with my pet for at least 15 minutes.
- [ ] I brushed my pet.

Exercising

"Do you ever feel lazy and not want to do anything? That's exactly why we are going on an adventure to a planet with a problem. This planet's aliens don't feel like exercising or playing sports and it's making them lazy. We have to help them remember how fun it is to play sports and get some simple exercises everyday. Let's see how we can get this planet back into shape so they can be healthier and happier."

Dear Jinga

We need your help!

The Star-Bazlooz are so lazy. None of them are exercising or even playing sports. We need to get them back to being healthy and active.

Thank you!
The leaders of the Star-Bazlooz

"Hello, Star-Bazlooz, your leaders are worried that you have stopped exercising and playing sports."

"Hello, Jinga! We are fine. Join us, we are going to spend the day having long naps. We just love having our naps."

"May I join you today?"

"Yes...follow us."

I love recess!
Me too!
Nap time!
Snore

I wish the fridge was closer.
Me too...

I am too lazy to walk to school. I will roll there.
SCHOOL

"Well, Star-Bazlooz, like your leaders, I'm worried about your health.

"Jinga! We just like to rest."

"Sleep is important for our health, but exercising is just as important. Will you follow me now?"

"Yes!" the Star-Bazlooz answered.

Jinga began to teach the Star-Bazlooz how to take care of themselves to become healthier. Together they skipped rope...

...they swam and learned that they loved it...

...they even moved the fridge back into the kitchen.

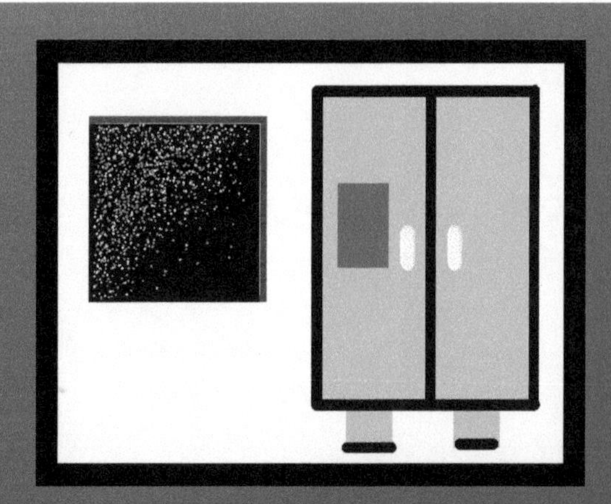

Jinga's
20 day Fitness Challenge:

10 Jumps	Touch your toes 12x	Take your pet for a walk	Hop on your right foot	Dance to your favorite song
Hop like a frog	Walk to school	Walk like a crab	Take the stairs instead of the elevator	Ride your bike
Skip for 30 seconds	Swim	Hula hoop for a minute	Walk to school	Bounce a ball for as long as you can
Rake the leaves	Sweep the floor	Hop on your left foot	Reach for the sun	Bounce a ball

Be Kind

"Has anyone ever been unkind to you? Has anyone ever called you a name? Have you ever been unkind to someone? We are going to help a planet that has become unkind to one another. We have to help them learn how to be kind by accepting others, treating others how we want to be treated and to remember how we feel when we are being treated unkindly. Let's see how we can get this planet back to being kind so that everyone feels safe and happy."

Dear Zeek:

We need your help!

Our schools are having problems with students being unkind. Can you teach our students how to be kind?

Thank you!
The Keen-Tahs

"Zeek? From The Dazingaz? Why are you here?"

"Keen-Tahs, your leaders have called me because they would like me to visit your school and spend the day. May I join you?"

"Sure the bell is about to ring!"

Give me the ball now!
Ha ha! He dropped his crayons!
Why are you so short and blue? You look funny and different.

After spending the day at school with the Keen-Tahs,

Zeek knew he had to quickly teach them the

difference between being kind and unkind.

How do you feel when someone is not kind to you?
It makes me sad. I don't like it.
How do you feel when someone is kind to you?
It makes me feel happy.
How does it make you feel when you do something kind for someone?
It makes me feel happy that I could help someone.
When you were being unkind how did it make you feel?
I know I'm not being kind. It's not the right thing to do.

Let's try and fix how we can all be kinder today.

Kind	**Unkind**
Caring	
Shares	Mean
Gentle	Doesn't share
Nice	Not friendly
Friendly	Loud
Sensitive	Doesn't listen
Warm	Lies
Honest	
Thoughtful	
Good	
A good listener	
Helpful	

Can I play
with you?

Here...

I like that we
look different.

Donating Clothing & Toys

"Have you ever really, really wanted a toy but you weren't allowed to get it? We are going to help a planet that has forgotten the difference between NEEDS & WANTS. We have to help them learn that wants are not as important as needs, and some people on the planet can't even get basic needs to live comfortably. Let's help them distinguish needs & wants and donate those things that they no longer use or need. Let's see how we can get this planet back to where everyone has their basic needs met."

Dear Kali:

We need your help!

Some of our Zat-Laz like to buy everything they want. Now they have so many toys and clothes that they do not use anymore. Their closets and homes are full. Where can we put all these things?

Please help us.

Thank you
The Zat-Laz

"Hello Zat-Laz, it is wonderful to meet you. What seems to be the problem?"

"Hi Kali. We have so many things and have run out of places to put them. We heard you are the best at organizing."

Kali went and visited some homes of the Zat-Laz.

Kali realized this was not a mission about organizing, it was much more. This was about teaching the difference between wants versus needs.

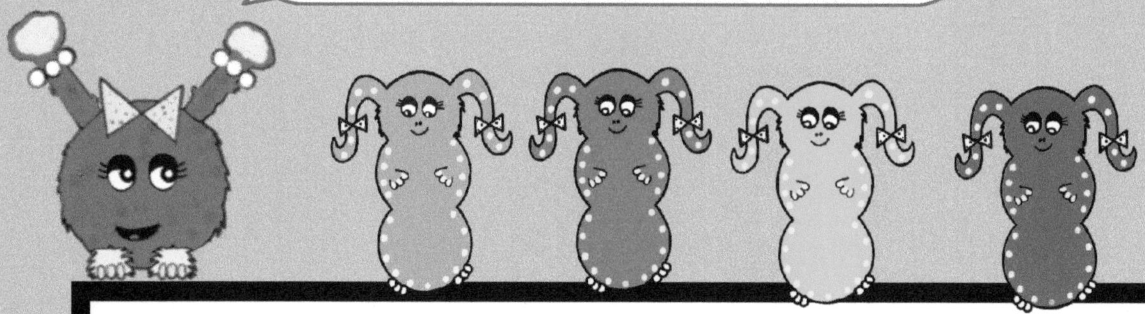

Wants Vs. Needs

Needs	**Wants**
Things we need to survive. -Food -Clothing -Shelter -Water	Things we like to have, but don't need to survive. -Cell Phone -Candy -A pet -Toys

After going through the list of needs and wants the Zat-Laz learned much of what they had were wants. Kali set up boxes that the Zat-Laz could use to organize their things: things that they used and things that they did not use anymore. The things they did not use would be sent to the shelter to be reused. Many of the things that they donated to the shelter were clothes and toys.

"Thank you, Kali! We will keep going through our closets and sort our toys, games and clothes. We will donate some of it to different charities."

Reusing helps us reduce the amount of trash in landfills in our universe.

What will you reuse today?

Recycle, Reduce and Reuse

"Do you recycle at home, school and other places in your community? Join me on my adventure to a planet that has never recycled, reduced or reused. They need help because the garbage is taking over their planet and the streets are getting ugly to look at and the smell is gross. I will help them organize what they will reuse, show them what they will reduce and of course how to recycle items. Let's see how we can get this planet back to being a place without piles of garbage and a stinky smell!"

We need your help!

Our planet has not been recycling, reducing or reusing, and now we have a big problem with piles of garbage. We don't know what to recycle, reuse or reduce. Where do we start, R3?

Thank you!
The Jum-Binos

It wasn't hard for R3 to see the piles of garbage. It looked ugly and it smelled bad.

"May I join you for the day?"

"Yes, please do!" said the Jum-Binos.

R3 followed the Jum-Binos and took note of some of the reasons why the planet was filled with garbage.

R3 has to teach the Jum-Binos how to recycle, reuse and reduce before garbage completely takes over.

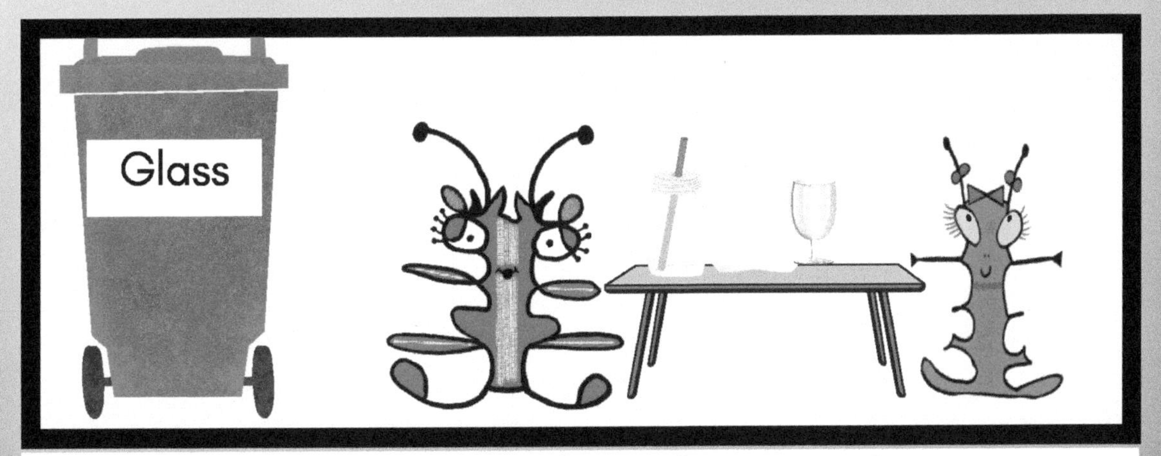

R3 taught about separating things that were glass.

R3 separated plastics.

R3 separated metal items.

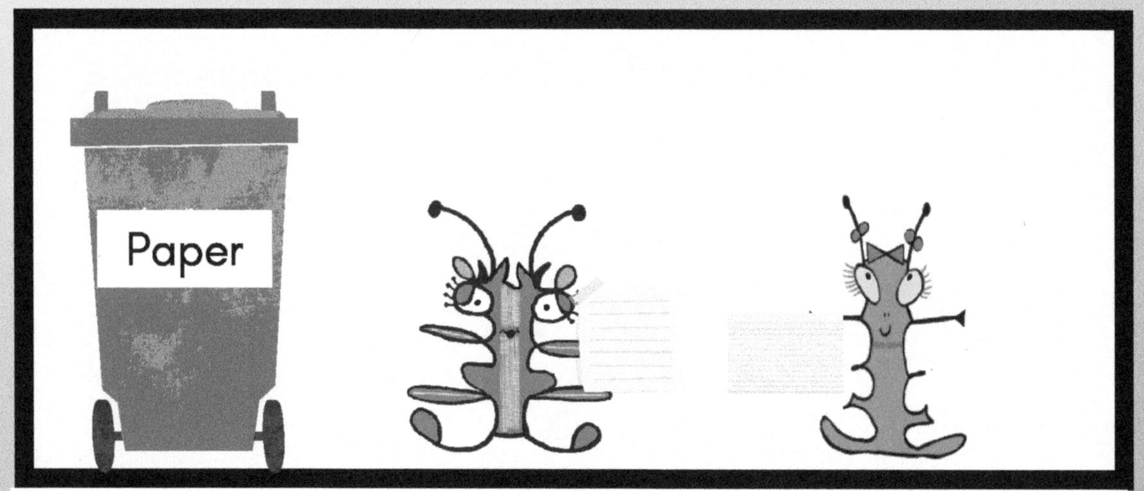

They looked for paper and put it into the paper recycling bin.

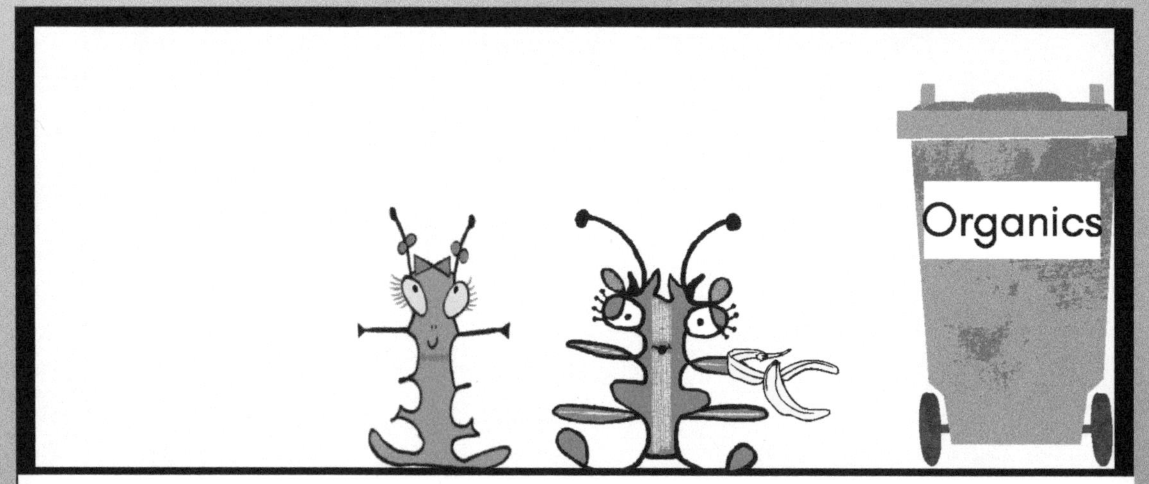

Next, the Jum-Binos separated organics, like food leftovers.

Then, the Jum-Binos separated e-waste (like small electronics).

Why do we need to do all of this?

Glass does not decompose into the earth. It stays in our dumps for a long time.

Plastics (containers, bags) like water bottles can take up to 450 years to decompose. Plastics are lightweight and easily blow away into our oceans and streets.

Metal (iron, copper, steel and aluminum) things like soda cans, keys and cans will leak dangerous chemicals into our planets' soils.

What do you recycle in your home?

- ☐ **Glass**
- ☐ **Plastics**
- ☐ **Metal**
- ☐ **Paper**
- ☐ **E-Waste**
- ☐ **Organics**

R3 and the Jum-Binos worked hard and it made a difference. Most of the garbage piles were actually items that could be recycled.

6

Shelter

"What kind of home do you live in? A house, condo, townhouse, trailer or a hut? We all need some form of shelter to keep us warm and safe. I need to go and help a planet that needs help because they don't have enough shelter for everyone to stay safe. Join me on my adventure to a planet where we will learn about why they need emergency shelter that I will help them build."

Dear Tago:

We need your help!

Our planet is changing & the weather becomes very cold. We don't have shelter to keep us warm or protect us.

Thank you!
The Noggle-Wiki's

"Welcome to our planet!" said the Noggle-Wiki's.

"Thank you. Your planet is beautiful and warm." Tago replied.

"That's the problem. Our world used to be warm every day, but

now there can be days with snow."

So, Tago stayed for a week.

Every day for six days the sun came out and it was warm. Warm enough to sleep at the beach!

On the last day, the weather changed. Tago, along with the Noggle-Wiki's, spent the night shivering and cold without any shelter.

Tago taught the Noggle-Wiki's how to use tools to build shelter.

The shelters kept the Noggle-Wiki's cool during the hot days...

...and warm during the cold ones.

Eat Healthy and Share

"What is your favorite food? Everyone loves food but sometimes on most planets food gets wasted. Join me on my adventure to a planet that has this problem. They have too much food and it's starting to rot. Let's go find a way to help them find a way to not waste all this amazing food."

Dear Seva:

We need your help!

Our planet is able to produce so much food that we are running out of places to put it. Do you have any ideas on where we can put all this food?

Thank you!
The Lo-Go-Yums

"Hi Seva, thank you for arriving so quickly! We need your help.

Our food grows so fast on our planet that we are always having

to throw so much away because it goes bad.

Our food grows so quickly on our trees. We don't know what we can do with all the extra food.

We have baked, canned, steamed, stewed and even barbecued but we still cannot eat it all.

Our planet produces more food than we can eat. So we had no choice but to throw it out into space.

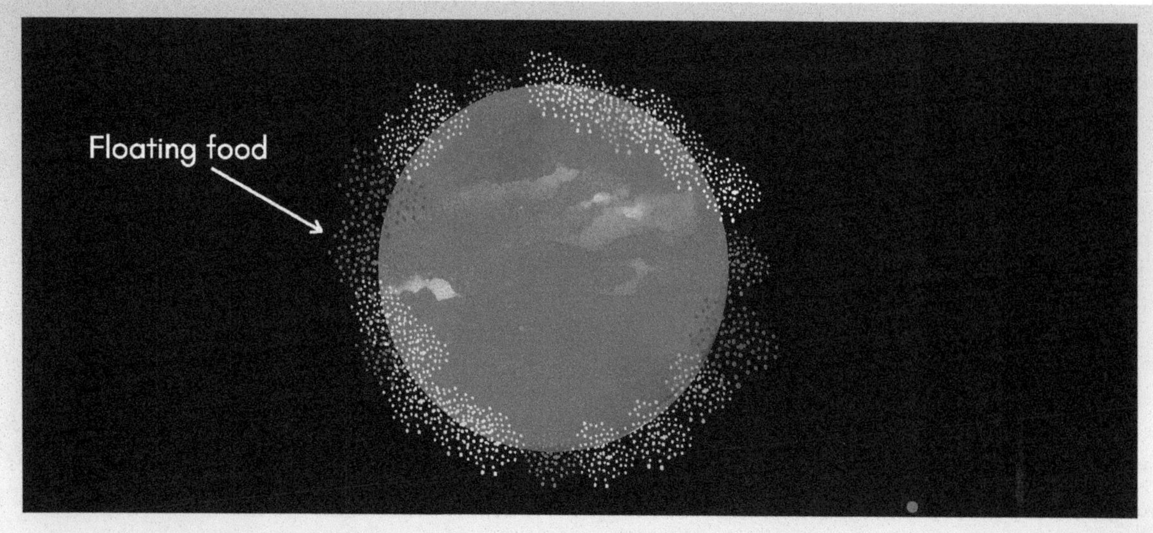

The extra food that your planet has been throwing out can be packed up and transported to another planet that needs it. This is called donating.
Donating food is giving food that you will not use and sharing it with planets that need it.

Here are some thank you letters from the planets you donated to.

"This makes us feel happy that we are not wasting food and

helping others!" Said the Lo-Go-Yums.

Dear Dazingaz:

COME QUICK!
WE NEED YOUR HELP.

Thank you!
PLANET EARTH

BE KIND

ABOUT THE AUTHOR

Amrita Sandhu is a kindergarten education assistant for the past 10 years in Vancouver, Canada. She loves sharing story ideas with her students and has been met with, "Ms. Rita...Can you write a book?!" So, she did just that. When she's not writing you'll find Amrita enjoying herself illustrating, cooking or eating candy.

Don't forget to leave a review on Amazon!

UPCOMING BOOK

LEARN MORE AT: WWW.THEDAZINGAZ.COM

CPSIA information can be obtained
at www.ICGtesting.com
Printed in the USA
LVHW071640020921
696802LV00005B/37